Why do stars come out at night?

A Red Fox Book

Published by Random House Children's Books
20 Vauxhall Bridge Road, London SW1V 2SA

A division of Random House UK Ltd
London Melbourne Sydney Auckland
Johannesburg and agencies throughout the world

1 3 5 7 9 10 8 6 4 2

First published in Great Britain by
Julia MacRae 1997

Red Fox edition 1998

Printed in Singapore

RANDOM HOUSE UK Limited Reg. No. 954009

ISBN 0 09 926456 0

Why do stars come out at night?

ANNALENA McAFEE

with illustrations by

ANTHONY LEWIS

Red Fox

Why is the sky so high?

Because the clouds would get caught in your hair.

Why do fish swim?

Because they've forgotten how to dance.

Why is the sea wet?

Because the mermaids wash their pearls.

Why is the grass green?

Because they ran out of blue.

Why is the sun hot?

Because it's been chasing around the earth.

Why do stars come out at night?

Because the moon is scared of the dark.

Why do we fall asleep?

Because our dreams must go out to play.

Why do babies cry?

Because they don't know how to sing.

Why do grown-ups get cross?

Because they haven't been kissed all week.

Why do children go to school?

Because teachers get lonely without them.

Why is the snow so cold?

Because the clouds forgot to wrap up.

Why are trees so tall?

Because they're trying to catch the birds.

Why do the birds fly?

Because they have to hold up the sky.

Why is the sky so high?

Some bestselling Red Fox picture books

THE BIG ALFIE AND ANNIE ROSE STORYBOOK
by Shirley Hughes
OLD BEAR
by Jane Hissey
OI! GET OFF OUR TRAIN
by John Burningham
DON'T DO THAT!
by Tony Ross
NOT NOW, BERNARD
by David McKee
ALL JOIN IN
by Quentin Blake
THE WHALES' SONG
by Gary Blythe and Dyan Sheldon
JESUS' CHRISTMAS PARTY
by Nicholas Allan
THE PATCHWORK CAT
by Nicola Bayley and William Mayne
WILLY AND HUGH
by Anthony Browne
THE WINTER HEDGEHOG
by Ann and Reg Cartwright
A DARK, DARK TALE
by Ruth Brown
HARRY, THE DIRTY DOG
by Gene Zion and Margaret Bloy Graham
DR XARGLE'S BOOK OF EARTHLETS
by Jeanne Willis and Tony Ross
WHERE'S THE BABY?
by Pat Hutchins